Not Now, Goldilocks!

For Muzzy, Boffy, Granny and Grandpa, who are
always there when Mummy is too busy – HR
To my lovely mom and dad, Rama and Mani – NR

Edited by Hannah Daffern and Susannah Bailey
Designed by Jack Clucas
Cover design by John Bigwood

First published in Great Britain in 2024 by Buster Books,
an imprint of Michael O'Mara Books Limited, 9 Lion Yard,
Tremadoc Road, London SW4 7NQ

W www.mombooks.com/buster f Buster Books 🐦 @BusterBooks 📷 @buster_books

Text copyright © Holly Ryan 2024
Illustration copyright © Navya Raju 2024, excluding colour work of pages 8–9, 14–15, 20–21, 26–27 and 32
Colour work of pages 8–9, 14–15, 20–21, 26–27 and 32 by Lisa Hunt, copyright © Buster Books 2024
Layout and design copyright © Buster Books 2024

A CIP catalogue record for this book is available from the British Library.

ISBN: 978-1-78055-968-1

1 3 5 7 9 10 8 6 4 2

This book was printed in July 2024 by Leo Paper Products Ltd,
Heshan Astros Printing Limited, Xuantan Temple Industrial Zone,
Gulao Town, Heshan City, Guangdong Province, China.

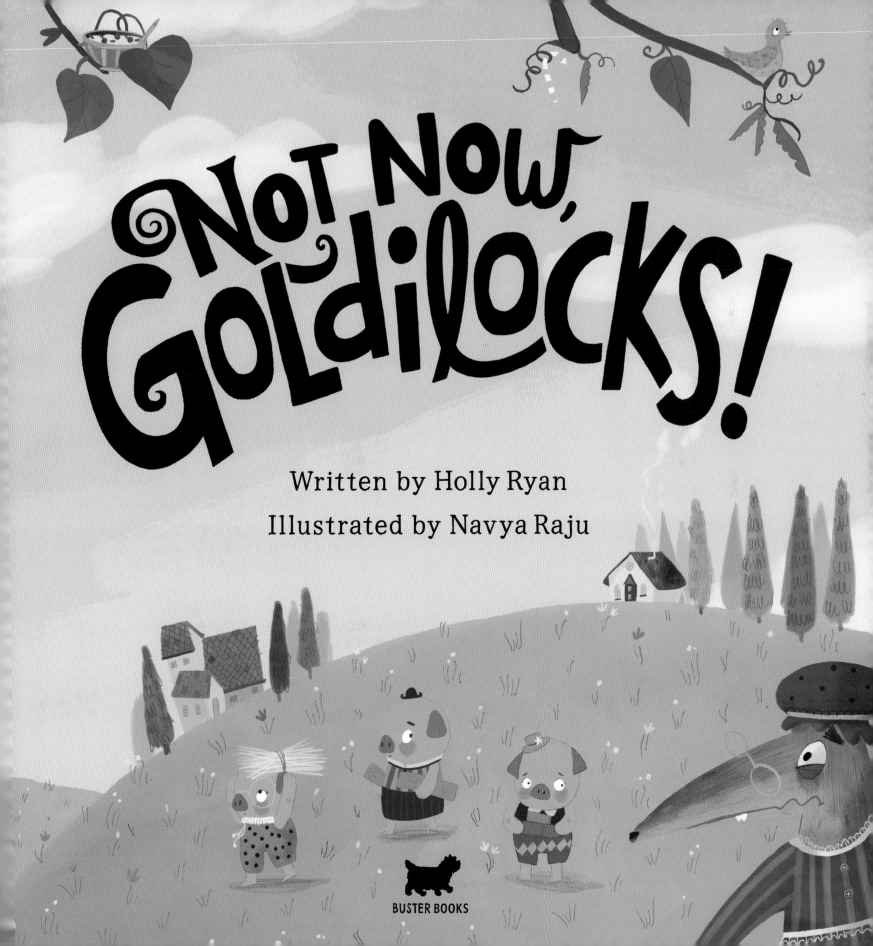

Not Now, Goldilocks!

Written by Holly Ryan

Illustrated by Navya Raju

BUSTER BOOKS

With pants over tights and a mask held with tape,
Toilet-roll laser and pillowcase cape,

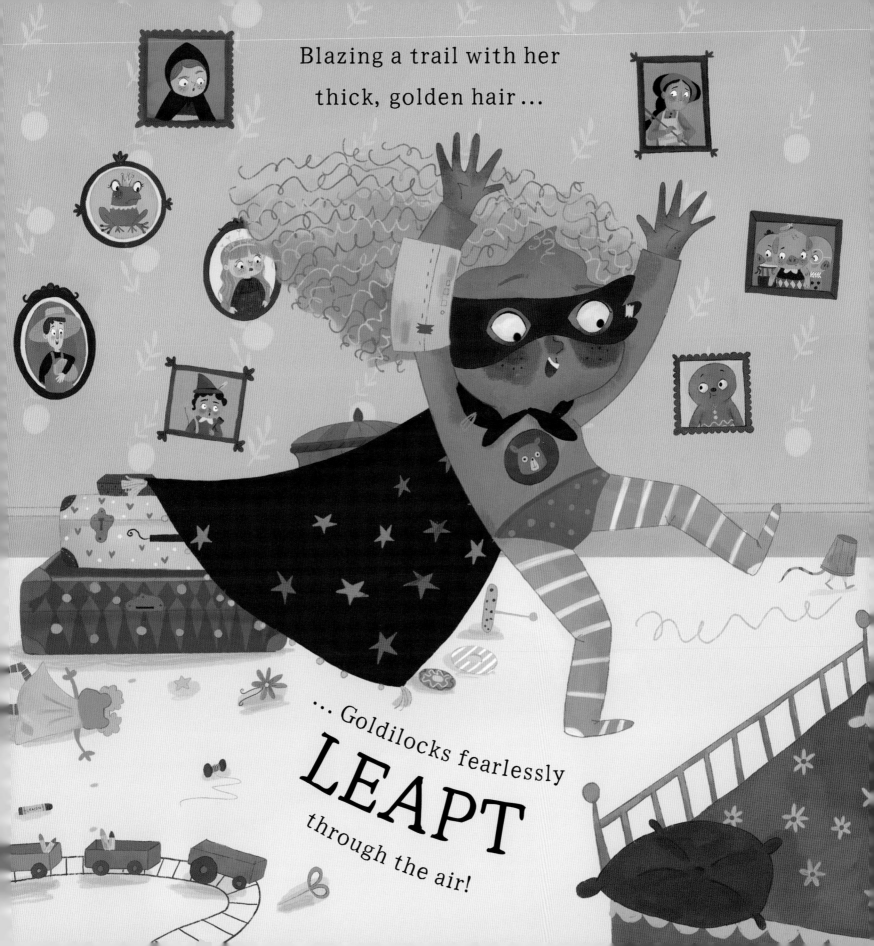

Blazing a trail with her thick, golden hair ...

... Goldilocks fearlessly
LEAPT
through the air!

"Fly with me, Mum, to the stars way up high,
We can build a tall rocket and WHOOSH through the sky!"

But Mum was too busy to fly to the Moon,
"Not now, Goldilocks, but we'll travel there soon.
I promise I'll play with you later today,
Perhaps Fairy Godmother's able to play?"

At Godmother's cottage, she found a large box,
And made a great sail out of blankets and socks.

Then Goldilocks made the most pirate-y ship,
"**QUICK**, Fairy Godmother, let's take a trip!"

Unfortunately, though, she was busy as well,
Mixing up potions and casting a spell.

"Not now, Goldilocks, there's just too much to do.

Like adding these worms to my new magic brew!

I'll play with you later, I promise," she said.

"Why don't you play with the neighbours instead?"

But Rapunzel was busy,
washing her hair . . .

And as for the bears,
they were fixing a chair!

And Robin and Red,
her two friends with the hoods,

Were chasing a wolf through a
DARK
SCARY
WOOD!

So,
Goldilocks
skipped
to the
palace
instead...

But found Sleeping Beauty asleep in her bed!

"This is ridiculous!" Goldilocks sighed.
Then out of the window she suddenly spied,
A towering beanstalk, and one grumpy giant,
And Jack with his battle-axe, looking defiant!

"I've made a new carriage, Jack! Fancy a spin?
There's plenty of room," she remarked with a grin.

"Not now, I'm too busy.
This beanstalk needs weeding,

And also that cute ugly
duckling needs feeding.

Why don't you play with Prince Charming instead?
I'll play with you later, I promise," he said.

But it looked like the prince was too busy as well,
Desperately ringing on everyone's bell.

And poor Cinderella had cleaning to do,
Which wasn't that easy with only one shoe!

"Not now!" she said busily,
shaking her head.

"Maybe just play on your
own," Cinders said.

So that is EXACTLY what Goldilocks did!
In armour she'd made from an old saucepan lid.

She leapt on her steed, which was Cinders' old mop,

And galloped about with a skip and a hop!

CASTLE

She raced through the village, and leapt over logs,

Pulled up a turnip and even kissed frogs!

FROGS

Goldilocks found that adventures for one,
Were really exciting, AND best of all ... FUN!

But what was that rustling high in the tree?

THE SCARIEST
DRAGON
YOU EVER DID SEE!

"Wow," whispered Goldilocks. "Look at those claws!
Am I soon to be lunch in those terrible jaws?"

But all of a sudden, with trumpets and ROARS!
Ready for battle, and finished with chores,
With shields they had made from some old odds and ends,
She spotted her mother, her neighbours, and friends.

And they fought that green beast for the rest of the day ... until it got tired and tiptoed away.

Squeezing her tightly, without letting go,
Mum said to Goldi, "I hope that you know,
I love you much more than the Moon way up high,
And more than the twinkling stars in the sky.

So I'll always make time for adventures," she said.

Then she planted a kiss onto Goldilocks' head.

Just before bedtime, they both built a rocket,
Made from some blankets and stuff from Mum's pocket.

They shot through the night, as the rocket went

ZOOM...

Then they both fell asleep...
On the top of the Moon.

THE END